When Is A Clock

by Matthew Freeman

SAMUEL FRENCH

FOUNDED 1830

NEW YORK HOLLYWOOD LONDON TORONTO

SAMUELFRENCH.COM

IMPORTANT BILLING AND CREDIT REQUIREMENTS

WHEN IS A CLOCK was first produced by Blue Coyote Theater Group (Kyle Ancowitz, Robert Buckwalter, Gary Schraeder, Stephen Speights) at the Access Theater in New York City from April 15th, 2008 – May 10th, 2008.

GORDON . . . . Tom Staggs

BRONWYN . . . . Tracey Gilbert

ALEX . . . . Beau Allulli

SEAN . . . . Ian Gould

CAROLINE . . . . Laura Desmond

COP . . . . David DelGrosso

LUCY . . . . Megan Tusing

CALDWELL . . . . Matthew Trumbull

Director . . . . Kyle Ancowitz

Stage Manager . . . . Susan Sunday

Sets . . . . Robert Monaco

Lighting . . . . Daniel Meeker

Sound . . . . Brandon Wolcott

Press . . . . Karen Greco

CHARACTERS

GORDON - a middle-aged man

BRONWYN - a middle-aged woman

ALEX - Gordon and Bronwyn's son

SEAN - who owns a bookstore in Cornersville

CAROLINE - a co-worker of Gordon's

COP - a Cop

LUCY - a young woman

CALDWELL - a co-worker of Gordon's

SET

Various settings, some real, some imaginary, in Pennsylvania.

AUTHOR'S NOTE

The text of ***WHEN IS A CLOCK*** was aided immeasurably by the dedication, insight and passion of Blue Coyote Theater Group; especially Kyle Ancowitz, director of the original production.

My thanks and love to Pam, whose eclectic tastes inspired much of this play's magic.

My apologies to Pennsylvania, where I was born, raised, and learned to love the theater.

*(Lights rise on **GORDON**, in his late forties or early fifties. He is not particularly hearty, and not particularly harmless. He speaks to us. He's puzzling it through, for us.)*

GORDON. I bloom. I molt. I get well. I get ill.

(pause)

My skin, when unattached, becomes dust. This dust is what my wife, when we were married, would clean from my shirts with soaps that, were I to drink, would kill me. After all that, I wore the shirts, then clean, and my skin came off all over them. With a little wind in the right places, the skin wound up attached to bookshelves, to the television set, to the floor. Everyone in my house would sneeze. I would check the pollen count in the spring, and blame flowers...just because I couldn't keep myself from shedding.

(pause)

One morning there was a book sitting on my wife's bed-side table. The book was by a writer from Oregon, who had driven around the country in a VW Bus in the 1970s. The bookmark seemed rather deep into the book.

(pause)

She had read almost the entire book, according to the green bookmark, without my having seen the book once. It also had no library card. It also had no dust jacket. So she had gotten from a flea market. Maybe. Maybe. Or she had borrowed it from someone. Maybe. Maybe.

(pause)

The book's binding was grey, the bookmark green. The bookmark, which I still have...

(He produces it, reads it to us:)

Prima Materia Books. There is no full address, only the name of a town. The town of Cornersville. No state. No giveaway.

(He turns to **BRONWYN,** *his wife.)*

Prima Materia Books?

BRONWYN. Hand that over.

GORDON. Where's Cornersville?

BRONWYN. Why? Are you taking a day trip?

GORDON. Is it somewhere I could drive?

BRONWYN. Depends on how much gas you have in the tank. Now give me my book.

GORDON. Is that where you got this book?

BRONWYN. No.

(pause)

I'm borrowing it. The bookmark was in it when I borrowed it.

(pause)

I'm almost finished with it, though. So I can give it back. So please give it back.

(She holds out her hand.)

GORDON. *(to the audience)* The things I didn't say include:
"Who are you borrowing it from?"
"Why didn't I notice this book before?"
"How long have you had it?"
"Is it any good?"

I won't say, for certain, that I should have asked these things. I simply know that I didn't ask these things. I just gave her the book. A week later...she was gone and did not come back.

*(***SEAN*** appears.)*

SEAN. Is there some reason you're just standing in front of my house?

GORDON. Is this your house?

SEAN. We've established that it isn't *your* house.

GORDON. So we have.

SEAN. Yes.

GORDON. And I'm standing in front of your house.

SEAN. Yes.

GORDON. Do other people live in your house?

SEAN. No.

GORDON. And there are no other houses around?

SEAN. Right.

GORDON. So why are we keeping our voices down?

(– to the audience –)

That house was in Cornersville. There is one house there that I found. And a barber. The grocery store, such as it is, is actually outside the town limits. It's barely a town. If not for the factory. They make copper wire. It's an industry that's being destroyed by fiber wire. But there you have it.

(pause)

Strictly speaking…there must have been more houses there. More people. Hidden, as one might say, in the brush. I never saw those other houses. Never saw those other people. Nevertheless, there may have been, or must have been, homes to be found in Cornersville besides that one, beside the factory, on Route 33, in front of a creek, just at the bottom of an incline.

BRONWYN. *(to GORDON)* What is completely satisfactory to me, completely, is the way in which you comb your hair. That's the best part of you. You comb it in this very organized way.

GORDON. *(to BRONWYN)* It never looks organized by the end of it.

BRONWYN. It would look like you were vain, if you were vain. But you're not vain. You just do it the way you know how to do it.

GORDON. My friend Jim, in Junior High, used two combs. Straight down each side, with a little gel.

BRONWYN. You know what I like about you? You're not Jim.

GORDON. Jim was a card. Never had much luck.

BRONWYN. When I was a little girl, I thought to myself, "I like a man who combs his hair."

GORDON. I comb my hair.

BRONWYN. We're star-crossed.

GORDON. I spit on brushes. My comb is my bond.

BRONWYN. How could I have known, when we met, that this could be so perfect?

GORDON. *(to the audience)* Connections between us were often uncovered this way. She was addicted to those little points where we were drawn together. Those synchronicities. She used to hate it when I would call us magnets, because magnets repel one another. She would say that I was iron and she was a magnet. That description, as a metaphor, felt better to say when we were in bed. It wasn't apt. In the long run, and the short run, and when standing still, it wasn't apt.

(pause)

You might well ask me, if you were the one speaking, why I so clearly remember the afternoon that my wife disappeared. Because time, for all its faults, is essentially the way we see things change. We barely notice it when things don't change.

*(**GORDON** sits at a desk. **CAROLINE**, a co-worker, approaches. She's around his age. Their banter is automatic, dispassionate.)*

CAROLINE. Thirty three. That's the figure, and they say "Take it or leave it."

GORDON. Fuck 'em if they can't take a joke.

CAROLINE. Exactly! Exactly. Now, what Jim said…you know Jim?

GORDON. The one from downstairs?

CAROLINE. Jim on Eight.

GORDON. So upstairs.

CAROLINE. Right. Jim on Eight. He said that we should take thirty-three, and just thank them for it and call it a day. He said if we get the contract then we'll have thirty-three now and that pretty much guarantees that we'll have a long future and more opportunities to hit higher numbers.

GORDON. Like ninety.

CAROLINE. Sure. Or seventy.

GORDON. Ninety hits the goal.

CAROLINE. Seventy is in line with projections.

GORDON. Thirty-three is nothing. I spit on it. I find it insulting. What would Jim say to that?

CAROLINE. He'd say think long-term.

GORDON. Between you and me. Between us. Between me and you. The problem with long-term thinking is that it tends to compromise the immediate victory. For example, we could absolutely, absolutely hit forty tomorrow if we asked for it. Especially if we mentioned seventy as what was projected. They're throwing thirty-three at us because they're expecting us to think long-term. What if we said "Fuck 'long-term.' Right now, we expect seventy." They'll give us forty.

CAROLINE. Hey, don't look at me. I don't work on Eight. That's their whole job. Can't expect them to do less than their job, can you? No. Not at all. They aren't allowed to think like we do, because they'd be fired for thinking like we do. Our job is to look at thirty-three and get insulted. Their job is to think about ninety in ten years. Somewhere in the middle we get sixty or seventy. But if it was just us or just them...what would it be? Chaos. That's why I stick to my department and so does Jim. Still though. Thirty-three? The wrong fucking way. Like all sane human beings, we piss upon it with our skirts up.

GORDON. If I were to order Thai, would you…

CAROLINE. Hell yes.

GORDON. Where is the bitch with the menus?

CAROLINE. That's downstairs Jim.

GORDON. I'm going to get coconut lime soup. That is what
    I get.

CAROLINE. I hate it when you get that. That's revolting.

GORDON. I know. I know you hate it.

CAROLINE. You're talking to a gal that gives deeper throat
    than Watergate and that shit makes me gag.

GORDON. You know what makes me gag? Jim. I spit on Jim.
    I spit on all men named Jim. When I was a kid, I had
    a friend named Jim who would comb his hair with two
    combs.

CAROLINE. Was he retarded?

GORDON. No. No, he was just trying to be unique.

CAROLINE. So he's in jail now, right?

    (pause)

GORDON. Yes, he's in jail now.

    (Elsewhere, **BRONWYN** *and* **SEAN***, not long ago.)*

BRONWYN. I'll go to jail.

SEAN. You'd never get caught. It works like this. You
    change. They see you, they say "Oh, how beautiful."
    They give us the money. You go, you stay, and when no
    one's looking…you come home to me.

BRONWYN. Then we do it all over again.

SEAN. Exactly.

BRONWYN. How many times?

SEAN. Until we've had enough. Until we've got enough.

    (pause)

    Until we're finished. Until you've had enough.

    (GORDON *continues speaking to the audience.)*

GORDON. When I got home that afternoon, I found my son
    eating Campbell's Soup directly out the can, without

even heating it up. He sucked soup into his mouth like an anteater at an anthill.

(Lights on **ALEX***, Gordon's son.)*

ALEX. Jesus Christ. Jesus Motherfucking Christ. One of the nuns today went off. She just went insane. Fucking shit she went insane. Ok, ok, ok, so we're just standing outside and Sister Ashkelon comes out and tells us that Saint George had milk for blood. Ok, yes. Good. We're listening because we have no choice, right? Then she says that the dragon that Saint George supposedly slays actually represents a pagan cult. And that Saint George was a Roman who fought in Turkey. Ok, whatever. Why tell us all this, right? What's the fucking point?

(pause)

Then she, right, she starts to tell us that there's this rated R version of it. That basically the dragon was offered a princess as a human sacrifice because if she doesn't get fed to him, then they can't have water in this town for whatever reason. And it's like 2 A.D., right? So they can't think of things to do to fix it. So they're like, "Short straw, Princess. Down the dragon's gullet."

(pause)

So this solider named George shows up from the Roman Army and he says, "You know what dragons dig? Tits." He takes off the Princess's bra, and then wraps it around the dragon's head and this whole thing hypnotizes the dragon and he winds up like, enchanted by her boob nets.

(pause)

Groovy. Then, right…this soldier leads the dragon back into town and what does he do? He totally shows off. He's like, "Take a gander, fellows and fellowladies. I am going to kill this totally zombified dragon, because I know how to handle a D cup." And then he kills the Dragon in the town square and everyone, I don't know, dances in its blood like Caligula and all that fun stuff. *This* is the story she tells us. This story about tits and stabbing stuff.

(pause)

Here's the obvious question. Should I whip it out for this nun? Because it appears as if she wants to get nailed.

GORDON. I ask him where his mother is. His lips, thin like mine, seemed unable to move in any direction useful, slaves to the whims of his head. I watch him and know that it was my genetic code that made him so uncontrollably idiotic. I also knew that, unlike my Father, I was soft and was raising my son as soft. My son would be unable to keep any job that was difficult, unable to pay much attention to things that did not, expressly, demand his attention. Recognizable as this behavior was, it was occurring to me, or starting to, that only through a sort of mild abuse would I cure him of this type of behavior. I wasn't strong enough to be abusive. Some men are too weak to be kind. Either or, none of us are completely good fathers. We can always be to blame.

(pause)

I asked him again: "Where is your mother?" He ate his soup. I went upstairs, watched a movie, and went to sleep. I woke up without my wife.

*(**GORDON** crosses to **ALEX**. They are at home, together, alone.)*

ALEX. Morning.

GORDON. Go to school.

ALEX. No school today.

GORDON. No school today?

ALEX. No. It's a holiday.

GORDON. Which one?

ALEX. It's Memorial Day.

GORDON. Oh.

ALEX. Didn't remember Memorial Day.

GORDON. Right.

ALEX. Want eggs?

GORDON. You have eggs?

ALEX. No, but you could make eggs. I want eggs. Do you want eggs?

GORDON. Sounds good.

ALEX. So…

GORDON. I'll make eggs.

(Years ago. **BRONYWN**, *elsewhere, speaks to* **GORDON**.*)*

BRONWYN. In the grand scheme of things…I'll always have only my eyes. My hands. My wrists. You read stories about women who can have orgasms by penetration alone, and women who get plastic surgery and you read about women who decide, these days, that marriage is this very old, traditional construct that has no basis in modern life. I'm none of those people. I can read about them, but I'm not them. I can't be them, and the only way I can even imagine what it's like is to read magazines and books and watch them on television. They can, in return, only imagine what it's like to meditate and believe in biorhythms and have hips that are actual size. I have just as much in common with a man who mediates as I do with a woman who's got her original nose. I know I'm supposed to feel a kinship with other women, automatically…but I don't. I mean, do you feel like just because someone is male, you automatically have some understanding of how they feel or felt? No. You feel a bond with whomever you identify with. That the sort of freedom I want. Thinking whatever I think no matter when I was born, where my genitals were grafted.

(pause)

Am I making sense?

GORDON. *(to the audience)* She did make sense. She said that on the night we first took a walk alone together. She said it in Philadelphia, in Fishtown. We were, despite my attempts to sabotage it, just about to fall in love. I had gotten yelled at by a cab driver, by the waiter. I had talked at length about something in the newspaper. An article I hadn't remembered right. It came out garbled. I barely listened to her all night. Then she said, "the grand scheme of things" and I decided, then and there, there and then, that I was going to be in love with her.

(pause)

A few days passed and she didn't come home. I called her cell phone and found that it was ringing in her bag, which was in the bathroom, on the sink. I picked it up, saw my own phone number on the display, and the stuck it into its charger. Just in case.

(Lights on **BRONWYN**. *Alone. Now. She speaks to us.)*

BRONWYN. The book is called *Traveling to Montpelier* and it's, as much as any book can be, non-fiction. Its non-fiction, but it has flourishes. The writers name is Daniel Wallers, if you're interested to know.

(pause)

Wallers writes like an alien visiting Earth. He describes Oregon, for example, as "one of those lonely places where nature is supposed to keep you company." Of writing checks he says: "You pick up this little slide and tear it out. It's got print on the front and back. You include your own print, and then write out the numbers in English." He wonders what checks look like in Spain, and what they look like in Romania. It occurs to you, when you read it, that you just assumed that checks were checks. Then you realize…they are checks, and Wallers is a misanthrope. Then you realize that he's transforming you into a misanthrope.

*(**BRONWYN** and **GORDON**, as before.)*

BRONWYN. Hand that over.

GORDON. Where's Cornersville?

BRONWYN. Why? Are you taking a day trip?

GORDON. Is it somewhere I could drive?

BRONWYN. Depends on how much gas you have in the tank. Now give me my book.

GORDON. Is that where you bought this?

BRONWYN. No.

(*pause*)

I'm borrowing it. The bookmark was in it when I borrowed it.

(*pause*)

I'm almost finished with it, though. So I can give it back. So please give it back.

(*She holds out her hand. She turns to the audience.*)

He gave it back to me. He didn't ask me who loaned it to me. I didn't tell him, because he didn't ask.

GORDON. Cornersville, Tennessee. Cornersville, Mississippi. Cornersville, Pennsylvania. There are three. We don't live anywhere near the first two. A few days of work and watching my son eat soup, and I was ready to find my wife.

(*A* **COP** *enters. He looks and acts like a cop, whatever cops are like. The* **COP** *regards* **GORDON** *with cop-like skepticism.*)

So how does this work?

COP. If you have a photo of your wife, that's a start.

GORDON. I do. Of course I do.

COP. Did she take anything with her when she…left?

GORDON. No.

COP. …nothing at all? She left her cell?

GORDON. Right.

COP. We'll create a file. If she's gone for more than a month, we'll obtain dental records. We'll do a credit check and check public records. There are lots of ways to track movement and behavior these days. We have computers.

GORDON. You need to check her teeth?

COP. Sometimes we do. Yes. She left her wallet?

GORDON. She did. She didn't even take any clothes.

COP. Not even the clothes she was wearing?

(pause)

GORDON. She was wearing an off-white blouse and a cream colored skirt and brown pumps. She put on a green scarf, tied with a pin. All of which was in the house, on the floor, when I got home.

COP. So she was…what? Naked? When she…left?

GORDON. Or she has clothes that…I don't know about.

(pause)

COP. I want to stress something to you before we go very far with this, because I know that sometimes people become really agitated and I get tired of explaining it. Especially after the fact. A few things. Number one, she might just come home. That happens. Number two, because she is an adult and not a minor, what has happened here isn't actually a crime. She's just not here. Despite what most perfectly nice husbands and wives think, there is nothing criminal about a grown woman not being where she's supposed to be. It's a crime for her to neglect your son, if you want to press charges of that sort. But this is simply the beginning of the idea that there *might* be a crime involved. You file a missing person's report and it says, "Listen, my wife might be dead. I don't know, but since she's not here and I can't find her, there *might* have been a crime."

(pause)

You see what I'm after? There isn't a crime. Not yet. Unless we find out you killed her yourself and are covering your tracks, or you're playing a game, or she stole things, or her absence is a sign that she was abused.

Things along those lines. It's like getting a clue to a crime that you're not sure has happened.

(pause)

Am I clear enough on this point?

GORDON. Do you want the picture now?

COP. Yessir.

GORDON. Are you married?

COP. I'm a public servant.

GORDON. *(to the audience)* The police officer had dandruff on his shoulders. People call them "flakes" but they look more like shavings. Like someone put a little cheese grater to his milky skull. He seemed to think I'd done something to my wife. Who was to say I hadn't?

*(**CAROLINE**, from the office, draws **GORDON**'s attention. She is with **CALDWELL**, their supervisor.)*

CAROLINE. Jesus, Gordon. We're all torn up about what's going on. Torn up. Torn to shreds.

CALDWELL. Hell yes. Hell yes. Christ, you take all the time you need. I tell you it's a terrible thing. My wife, if she ever went missing, I'd piss all over my pants. Immediately.

(pause)

So you take all the time you need.

*(He extends **GORDON** his hand. They shake.)*

GORDON. Thank you.

CALDWELL. Jesus. Wife gone poof. What do you say about that? Nothing, that's what. That's the worst thing I've ever heard.

GORDON. It might not be. She might be fine.

CALDWELL. She might be *dead.*

(pause)

Ok, ok. Well, you take all the time you need. Caroline's got the particulars. Stiff upper lip, as they say in the Navy.

(**CALDWELL** *nods uncomfortably and exits.* **CAROLINE** *and* **GORDON** *regard each other.*)

GORDON. Is there an office pool?

CAROLINE. About what?

GORDON. If I'll quit? Or crack? Or cry?

CAROLINE. That would be monstrous.

GORDON. Barry got half of his leg chopped clean through by a boat propeller. Came in looking like a cyborg. I personally put down twenty five dollars on him bleeding *within* the building.

(*pause*)

CAROLINE. There is a pool. Wager's on whether or not you killed her. I said you didn't. Did you?

GORDON. Would you say that, before this little exchange, you considered us friends?

(*pause*)

CAROLINE. You don't even know my cat's name.

GORDON. Juliet. Romeo was the turtle.

CAROLINE. Terrapin.

GORDON. Right.

CAROLINE. That's just a parlor trick. It's not like you cared about the cat, or me, or Romeo.

(*pause*)

I have friends. I don't dislike you, I don't consider you abhorrent. I don't think of you as someone I'd invite to my kid's bar mitzvah.

GORDON. You have a son?

CAROLINE. You know that I do.

(*pause*)

Don't you?

GORDON. (*to the audience*) That's how we left it at work. I never asked if we took a shot at ninety. The people on eight weren't about to budge, and even if they did, they were probably just going to budge to see if I'd killed my wife. Which I hadn't. I haven't.

(pause)

The police were not helpful. They said that it would take a month before they'd need dental records. My son didn't say anything. What, I thought, is the sort of child who politely refuses to mention the loss of his own mother? The sort of child I raised personally, as it appears.

(The **COP** *speaks to* **GORDON**.*)*

COP. Crime statistics. The average person is married twice, and the average marriage contains seven steps, and the average marriage has around two children and the average child of those marriages spends an average of four hours watching two to four television programs on five nights a week. More than half of that time is spent watching violent crime, and of the twelve courtroom dramas currently dominating the networks prime time slots, they watch 276 variations of criminal actions, based on a 23 episode season. That is only counting the central act of criminality within the drama, not counting ethical lapses or more minor crimes in support of, or to dispel, the central crime in question.

(pause)

When, when, when you expose one half of one half of all Americans to four hours of around three hundred murders, rapes, kidnappings and assaults over the course of a season of television, you're going to create precisely, and we have this figure available on our website, around 500,000 potential major felons a night, of which exactly 45,678 will commit crimes within ten years of right now.

(pause)

How should we find your wife? With all this happening just because of television?

(pause)

What about red tape? And just *overall* numbers? Every second, 200 babies die in this county alone. 200. *Babies.* Die. In this county alone. Three hundred people lose watches every ten minutes in 38 states. There are 20 different versions of the law that protects three different ethnicities from twelve kinds of discriminatory lending practices. Food poisoning, from nearly 600 controlled substances, just hit the digestive system of two women. As we spoke. Their names are Janet and Janet. Both of them named Janet. What are the odds? Actually, very, very good, if you consider how improbable a life-sustaining atmosphere even is.

(pause)

89 times, in the course of just walking in this door, I envisioned a crime committed against me by a person that worked in an orphanage when I was only nine. Why do I see that in my mind so often? Biological signals sent from my brain, sense-memory? 91 times now. It just keeps happening. That person was never arrested, but was killed. You can't prove how. How could you? There's just too much to keep track of.

(pause)

Over the course of the last month, it was discovered that people's names were being spelled in a wantonly confusing manner by a large number of ethnic minorities in order to confound governmental databases. You think it's easy to track people by way of their social security number? Of course *you'd* think so. That's because you don't know that there are two million people in this country whose social security number is precisely the same as two million other people. How do you think that affects their records when they die? It's not pretty. Of course it's not pretty. In fact, despite what you may believe, according to Federal Databases, because of this Social Security glitch, more than half of those four million people are deceased.

(pause)

14 million Mexicans just entered this country. 15 million. 16 million. All without social security numbers, most of them less than 5 feet 5 inches tall. How are we going to find them and bury them? Do we just toss them in the Pacific Ocean? No, no we don't. That's how we hope to fuel agriculture. But there are so, so many. So many.

(pause)

Where is your wife?

GORDON. Pennsylvania.

COP. How, for fuck's sake, can you be so sure?

(pause)

GORDON. *(to the audience)* I decided to look for her myself.

*(Enter **LUCY**. She's young. Small. She is in a motel, out of bed, in a bra.)*

LUCY. You don't even try to hide it.

GORDON. Would it matter to you?

LUCY. Yes. I mean, if you hid it and then I found it. You think I'm this completely…whatever. This person who wouldn't care, but I'm not like that at all.

GORDON. If it matters to you, then you should go home.

LUCY. I don't want to go home.

GORDON. That's really up to you.

(pause)

LUCY. What do you do?

GORDON. When? When I'm not here?

LUCY. Right. What do you do when you're not at the Days Inn?

GORDON. My department sells ad space in periodicals for tourism. Marketing pieces for hotel lobbies and ticket counters. We get low-balled and then the geniuses upstairs tell us to take it.

LUCY. So you don't do anything.

(pause)

LUCY. *(cont.)* I mean, you don't make anything. You sell things. You're a salesman.

(pause)

My family has a business that makes soap. Fancy soap. We sell it at the farmer's market.

GORDON. The flea market?

LUCY. No, there's a farmers market, it's like huge. Biggest one in the county. Mennonites and junk shops and stuff. I work over there and hang out at the bar.

GORDON. So you don't work at the factory.

LUCY. That's for townies.

GORDON. You're not a townie.

LUCY. We moved here from New York when I was eleven.

GORDON. How old are you now?

LUCY. That would be telling.

(pause)

You're divorced?

GORDON. No.

LUCY. So you're cheating.

GORDON. Have you ever been to a store called *Prima Materia Books*?

LUCY. Yeah. Sure.

GORDON. You have?

LUCY. Yeah.

GORDON. Is it near by?

LUCY. It's on Hurlinger's off of Route 33. Can I see your ring?

GORDON. No. And you also can't touch it, if you can help it.

(– to the audience –)

I pulled over to buy an apple. That's something I never really get to do where I live. There aren't "apple stands" next to fields, next to open roads. Lucy was there, and she took a big shiny bite of an apple and wiped the white juice off her chin. So I took her back to my hotel room and put a towel under her ass.

(**BRONWYN** *and* **SEAN***, elsewhere.*)

SEAN. Sometimes, when we're both awake and pretending to sleep, I see this parade in my mind. It starts off as counting sheep, and then the sheep are accompanied by wolves, and the wolves by little girls in red dresses, and they are followed by police officers and the police officers are followed by priests in vestments, and then the priests explode into any number of religious orders, and then the orders slaughter the sheep and carry the bloody sheep down the street, holding them over their heads, the blood covering the faces of Little Red Riding Hood and being lapped up by the wolves and the police officers are surrounding this parade with yellow tape. I see this and you are pretending to sleep. I know you're awake. We're both awake.

GORDON. *(to the audience)* I imagine my wife in the throes of another man's charms.

SEAN. The parade isn't a parade, anymore than anything is anything, when it's inside my mind. They say memories are these stored things, but instead, the past is this changeable, synthetic mish-mash. What I was is nothing, and I'm there, looking at the ceiling, or maybe a fake framed painting in my bed room, that one by Winslow Homer, and I feel old and distant and as if this nothing, this past, is totally confining me. Even though it doesn't exist.

GORDON. Where is she? Who is this girl I just fucked?

SEAN. There's something happening. To me. To you. Trees bow towards us when we walk together. The constellation Orion has ceased to exist. Flies grow spontaneously from garbage and rotting meat. Genetic research invents a cabbage with the mind of a dolphin. My muscles atrophy. Your husband sleeps with a woman half his age. Your son dies in a tragic accident. We blow cumulonimbus clouds from the bottom of our lungs onto unsuspecting strangers. The earth's temperature suddenly becomes completely stable and refuses to change. All the Catholic Saints visit a single woman in Pakistan, who has no idea who they are.

(pause)

All these things are happening to you. To me.

GORDON. Lucy and I had breakfast. Have breakfast.

LUCY. *(at a table at a diner)* You don't like it here.

GORDON. *(joining her)* I like it fine.

LUCY. You don't. It's ok. It's a dump.

GORDON. It's fine.

LUCY. That's what they call it around here. It's called "The Apple Dumpling" so everyone calls it "The Dump." It's where people come after football games and baseball games and the junior prom.

GORDON. Where do they go after the real prom?

LUCY. The Jersey Shore. It's just what people do.

GORDON. That's interesting.

LUCY. No it isn't. But it's true.

(She takes a stab at her food.)

You ever had scrapple?

GORDON. When I was younger. I can't get it where I live now.

LUCY. I like it with maple syrup.

GORDON. That sounds revolting.

LUCY. You don't like me

GORDON. Yes I do.

LUCY. Do you like your wife?

GORDON. Yes, I like my wife.

LUCY. Is it ok to ask about your wife?

GORDON. It isn't really.

LUCY. What's her name?

GORDON. Bronwyn.

(pause)

It's Welsh.

LUCY. Fine. That's what it is. It's a weird name. I don't like it. I would never name my daughter Bronwyn.

GORDON. To each his own.

LUCY. Her own.

GORDON. Her own.

LUCY. You know I don't have any money. To pay for breakfast.

GORDON. I know that.

(pause)

GORDON. *(to the audience)* It was time for Lucy to go home. I put her in the car. She talked for a long time about Kurt Vonnegut. He died you see. She told me like I didn't know.

(pause)

She seemed especially naïve, the way she looked out the window when she talked. She looked at the trees. I don't really look at trees. I've seen them. Or, if not those trees in particular, lots of trees. They bore me. She was intently watching each thing that we drove past as she talked about the *Sirens of Titan*. Our time was over and I could tell that I had I disappeared and the fact that I'd rolled her onto her stomach the night before had disappeared.

(pause)

So it goes. I pulled right up to the driveway as if I was dropping her off after field hockey practice. Her father stuck his head out the door and waved at me. It was the common wave of someone engaged in neighborly conduct. "Thanks for dropping her off!" he seemed to be saying. "Don't worry, we have tons of morning after pills and abortion clinics abound."

*(**ALEX** and **GORDON**, on the phone.)*

ALEX. Hey.

GORDON. Yeah?

ALEX. Hey.

GORDON. I'll be home soon.

ALEX. Got it.

GORDON. Are you all right?

ALEX. Yeah.

GORDON. Sorry I…left you at home.

ALEX. Well, it's not like you didn't leave any food.

GORDON. Is everything ok?

ALEX. No.

GORDON. No?

ALEX. I'm going to wind up in therapy and probably never have a happy marriage.

(pause)

GORDON. But otherwise.

ALEX. I'm spit-shined.

GORDON. Great. Be home soon.

ALEX. Fuck you.

GORDON. Bye.

(– to the audience –)

I'm getting ahead of myself. I thought that I should probably call Alex, but I decided to wait. It's not like that conversation would be fruitful. I looked for Hurlinger's Road, which is where Lucy said I might find the bookstore.

(pause)

Hurlinger's runs East-West and Route 33 runs North-South. When I hit it I had no idea in which direction to turn the car.

(pause)

There are many, many ways to solve this problem. But I went West. I turned the car to the West because the West is where the sun sets and the West just sounds good on paper. I drove West, taking a left turn.

(pause)

Hurlinger's Road is not a road, but, in fact, an

extension of a larger route that runs from Southeastern Pennsylvania, past Harrisburg, and then takes you up and north of Pittsburgh before depositing its riders en route to Cincinnati.

(pause)

It winds a bit, curls under a few bridges and hooks hard rights around old stone farmhouses, deep set in the woods. It didn't take long before, heading west, I had left Cornersville and traveled through a variety of villages and town-lets. Places like Haverstaad, Camps Glade, Parliament Township and Abnerton. Empty places, whose town borders existed only in the imagination of gerrymanderers. Still, they were indistinguishable from one another, and in being so, were ultimately numbing and kind to me.

(pause)

Of course I turned around, in accordance with all the laws of detective work, towards more fertile territory. In another story, one with a happier ending, I keep driving until I find a new job and a little place to live and am never seen again.

BRONWYN. *(to the audience)* I asked Sean why he had asked me to read *Traveling to Montpelier*. Sean explained that he had been given an unpublished chapter of the book. One that Wallers had released only to those who might not discount it outright.

*(**GORDON** and **BRONWYN**, together, years ago.)*

GORDON. I still love you.

BRONWYN. Someday my ass is going to expand.

GORDON. I'll still love you.

BRONWYN. There are going to be times when we don't have sex.

GORDON. I'll still love you.

BRONWYN. One of us will develop a problem with shitting.

GORDON. I'll still love you.

BRONWYN. We'll start to hunch over. Go blind.

GORDON. I'll still love you.

BRONWYN. I'll stop loving you.

GORDON. I'll still love you.

> *(pause)*

> I don't like these pillows. They're too big. They're killing my neck.

> *(pause)*

> Human beings are actually supposed to slouch, you know. The fastest way to a damaged lower back is to try to stand up straight all the time.

> *(pause)*

> I think there're going to promote Karen at work and I just don't get it. I mean, she's going to have my title. Our org chart is totally confusing. We need to hire someone in HR that knows what he's doing.

> *(pause)*

> I think we should get new pillows.

> *(pause)*

> Are you awake?

BRONWYN. *(to the audience)* I first met Sean just after Gordon and I were married. He didn't live that far away, maybe an hour into Dutch Country. We were still in Philadelphia then. It was a long time ago. Sean would call me, lend me things to read. For a while, it worried me. Then it stopped worrying me.

> *(pause)*

> When he came to get me, finally, it was because I asked him to.

GORDON. *(to the audience)* I came back around and found that only perhaps one mile *east* of Route 33, was *Prima Materia Books*. It was a modest purple shack with a white sign and sitting out front were three hippies in sweatshirts.

(pause)

I drove past it, and found a restaurant. I was starving.

BRONWYN. *(continuing)* I'll read you a little bit of the missing chapter…

"How many men must tie his shoelaces at once in order to make the sun turn into a block of ice? There is a number that adds up to this. There are a number of oranges we must eat, and there is a fruit that must be eaten next, if we are to invent an extra planet."

GORDON. *(continuing)* Hammering through some french toast, which I only ever eat with a pat of butter, it occurred to me that the only thing worth eating in the entire state of Pennsylvania was breakfast food. The Pennsylvania Dutch have starch and pig for dinner; tin plates filled up to the brim with breading and potted meat, and the only thing they did right, only thing, was scramble eggs and repeatedly pour coffee. They couldn't even make a burger right. They were the idiot children of a once proud state, and they were the secret lovers of the KKK in the North. No wonder they ate like shit.

(pause)

Is this where she went? How do I even actually know? Maybe I just felt like driving this way. Maybe she's buried somewhere near the house.

(pause)

I shoveled it all down and had an extra cup of coffee. It seemed to be getting late, which made no sense, and so I thought about places to sleep.

BRONWYN. *(as before)* Hand that over.

GORDON. Where's Cornersville?

BRONWYN. Why? Are you taking a day trip?

GORDON. Is it somewhere I could drive?

BRONWYN. Depends on how much gas you have in the tank. Now give me my book.

GORDON. Is there where you got this book?

BRONWYN. No.

(*pause*)

I'm borrowing it.

GORDON. Did you cut yourself?

BRONWYN. No.

GORDON. Your chin.

BRONWYN. Oh. When did this happen?

GORDON. (*to the audience*) Certain things don't happen in order, or they never happened, or I've forgotten them.

(*pause*)

Driving back to the motel took only a few minutes. After all that hubbub, it was clear that the Apple Dumpling and *Prima Materia* and the motel weren't that far apart at all. In fact, if you were looking at a road atlas, they'd all be in the same place.

(*pause*)

I returned to the scene of the crime and got the same room that I'd had the night before. Nostalgia doesn't take long to get its hooks in, now does it?

(*pause*)

The place was the same, but of course, devoid of any evidence of me or of Lucy. Or anyone. I rubbed a little of my dandruff into an empty drawer. Just to leave something.

(**SEAN** *and* **GORDON**, *outside of the house.*)

SEAN. How long are we going to stand out here talking?

GORDON. It could be hours.

SEAN. Let's not let it be hours. Let's get it over with.

(*pause*)

There is a part of the brain that makes people more *aware* of others. The empathy chip maybe. Some people have all sorts of activity in this area of the brain. It's said that's where the idea of telepathy comes from.

The reverse is a *deficiency* in this area. A deep loss of understanding. We open our idiotic mouths and our peers burst into stifled laughter, we cannot conceive of how to win them over. We are, if we don't have this chip properly configured, entirely without a sense of how our actions affect others and why we're making them so incredibly unhappy.

GORDON. *(to the audience)* In the motel, I slept the way one could expect to sleep. Somewhere was my wife, who I had, not for the first time, been unfaithful to. I felt someone had done something to her, or with her. Was even doing so at that very moment. That somewhere, she had a mouthful of chocolate cake, and she was laughing, frosting on her nose, like a kid at her eighth birthday party. The thought of her being so happy, so young, made my throat tighten. Why should she get to feel young?

(pause)

The next morning, I went back to the Apple Dumpling and ordered breakfast. The bookstore wasn't open yet. I didn't call Alex. I bought a newspaper instead. On the cover, it said that a private American security firm that was working in Iraq had opened fire on civilians. It was just one more example of something, but I couldn't put my finger on it. I was eating scrapple and it tasted like joyful grey gristle. This is what the Pennsylvania Dutch do right: they make breakfast.

*(***BRONWYN*** and ***SEAN*** are together in his house. She's bleeding just a bit from her chin. He's tending to her.)*

BRONWYN. Don't you fucking even start.

SEAN. Calm down.

BRONWYN. Look at my face. Look at it. I can't go back home now. Look at my chin.

SEAN. I'll get something for it.

BRONWYN. What the hell am I doing, Sean? This won't hold up in court.

SEAN. What happened?

BRONWYN. Everyone was asleep. I was myself again. I was going to call you to come and get me. But for some reason, his wife was up at 4 am, pulling weeds or some shit. She's holding this spade, and she sees a woman, me, wearing her husband's clothes running out of her house. So what do you think she does? She screams and takes a chunk out of my chin.

SEAN. Hold it. Hold it.

(**SEAN** *starts dabbing at her chin with hydrogen peroxide and a cloth.*)

BRONWYN. Fuck.

SEAN. Hold your head back.

BRONWYN. *You* hold it back.

SEAN. Stop moving.

BRONWYN. All I could think about is that now, now I was going to be caught. I'm caught. I can't go home now. I can't even think about going home now.

SEAN. How caught are you? You're not caught. You're home. You got here, safe and sound. Hold your head back. Don't panic. Shut up. Let me help you.

BRONWYN. What are we doing?

SEAN. …making some money?

BRONWYN. So that we can do what?

SEAN. Bronwyn. Listen. This isn't how things go around here. I don't like all this…yelling.

(*pause*)

BRONWYN. Wash it out.

(**SEAN** *quietly washes the cut out for a bit. As he does this,* **GORDON** *speaks.*)

GORDON. The waitress asks if I want my bill, but I'm only halfway through the *Inquirer* so I ask if it's ok if I just sit it out and stick around and order lunch. She's a portly older lady who has likely worked at this diner since the Enlightenment.

(pause)

I think about the bookmark, and the world of Pennsylvania and how I'm out on Route 33. Thirty three. Route 33. I spit on it. It insults me. That's what I think to myself.

(pause)

This is the only way I know how to follow breadcrumbs.

SEAN. There you go. See? It's going to be all right.

GORDON. I eat a Reuben, a rubbery one, slowly, drink more coffee, work my way through the papers. I've switched off of *USA Today* and onto the local paper, which is the *Abnerton Record*. Everything was about Abnerton. Cornersville seemed to have no local residents. Half of it was about how new developments are threatening the water table. There's an ad for the barber. There's a little map of the area, for some reason. Shows exactly where I am, but it's zoomed in close, so it's still hard to figure it all out. Local tribesfolk are furious that all the best young men aren't working in copper wire, which is the lifeblood of the local economy.

(pause)

Gray Wolf Copper. That's what the factory's called. I am, if the dream is to be believed, on the right track.

*(**GORDON** and **CALDWELL**, years ago. **GORDON** is interviewing for work.)*

CALDWELL. Welcome. Sit. Welcome. Caldwell.

GORDON. Hello Mr. Caldwell. Thanks. Sorry about the...

CALDWELL. Coffee on the tie? Coffee on the tie is par for the course. You play golf? That's a golf joke.

GORDON. I do not.

CALDWELL. Gotta learn. Gotta learn the golf. Your name is Gordon. That's a solid name. You Irish?

GORDON. Yes.

CALDWELL. You know that it wasn't all that long ago Irish
were treated like the blacks? That's the facts, Gordon.
Times change. You guys have potatoes and Bono.
You're kings. Blacks are another story. But you people
are kings. I watched that movie…*The Commitments?*
Remember that? Watched it fifty times. Must have.
Loved the music. Loved it. Always wanted to be in a
band. When I was younger. Now I work here for fuck's
sake. Chattel work. That's what I do now. Not singing
one lick.

(pause)

But I do have a golf swing that would put nuts on a
bitch. I'll tell you that right now.

(pause)

So you met Caroline?

GORDON. I did.

CALDWELL. You'd be working with her. She's a stitch. Hates
the guys upstairs. Everyone does, but that's the business. That's how things fly in the world. She came here
looking like that sort of woman and so she is. I am an
excellent reader of people. I knew right away where
she should work. We are what we are, and no more.
No less.

GORDON. So it goes.

CALDWELL. Do you eat fish? I'm allergic.

GORDON. I do. Sometimes.

CALDWELL. I'm allergic.

GORDON. I see.

CALDWELL. I had a dream, not very long ago, about cod.
The Atlantic Cod is in danger from over-fishing. I was
told this in the dream. A woman told me just before
she turned into a hat. She told me the literal and cor-
rect names for cod. The genus of cod. For example,
the Pacific Cod, I was told in my dream, is the *Gadus
macrocephalus*. It is also known as the gray fish or gray
wolf.

(*pause*)

Strange for it to be true, don't you think? I went to the Encyclopedia Britannica. Looked it up. All true. And of course, before my dream, I knew nothing of it. Completely allergic to fish. Hate them. They're like Kryptonite to good old me.

(*pause*)

Strange that I should tell you. About that. Isn't it.

GORDON. I guess so.

CALDWELL. Ah well. Pish posh. You're from Philadelphia. What the hell are you doing up here?

GORDON. I got married. I have a son.

CALDWELL. Son, eh? Carry on the family line, he will. If he's not gay. But then he could adopt, right? So all would not be lost. You wanted a son?

GORDON. Actually, I was hoping for a girl.

CALDWELL. Takes a big man to admit that. Big man. I'm glad I don't have a girl. I'll tell you that. I'd have her locked up in the attic, reading the Robert Ludlum. Jesus, Mary and Joseph. I know how men are. Trust me. I've been through sexual harassment courses. I know the sickness of the human heart.

(**BRONWYN** *speaks to* **GORDON** *as he turns to her. Years ago.*)

BRONYWN. (*laughing*) You're shitting me.

GORDON. That's what he said.

BRONWYN. The sickness of the human heart?

GORDON. That's what he said.

BRONWYN. The sickness of the human heart?

GORDON. Probably get it from playing golf.

BRONWYN. That's the best thing I've ever heard. That man must be on 24 hour suicide watch.

GORDON. I think he's going to give me a job.

BRONWYN. He owes you a job for that. He owes you.

GORDON. I don't want to work there.

BRONWYN. You don't want to work anywhere. At least it'll be hilarious. It's clearly hilarious. He's brilliant. If you do work there, I expect reports, weekly, on how depressing he becomes. I want to get video of him in sexual harassment courses. I bet it's a how-to guide.

GORDON. And so it came to pass that we met the good people of Erie, Pennsylvania.

BRONWYN. Don't start.

GORDON. And they were what we imagined them to be. Crass, empty of organs, rudderless hicks.

BRONWYN. Someday, I swear to God, you're going to smile about something that's funny.

GORDON. *(to the audience)* Her eyes had lit up. I did not tell her about Mr. Caldwell's dream. It didn't seem important then.

(The **COP** *approaches* **ALEX**, *at his home.)*

COP. Hey.

ALEX. What?

COP. Your dad home?

ALEX. He's dead.

> *(pause)*

> No, he isn't.

COP. You're Alexander?

ALEX. What are you?

COP. I'm a police officer.

ALEX. You can't come in here without a warrant.

COP. I'm not going to search the house. I'm looking for your father. He put in a missing person's report for your mother. Who, I take it, also isn't home.

ALEX. No.

> *(pause)*

> Not right now.

COP. Out to get a bottle of milk?

(*pause*)

No one makes milk in bottles in anymore. You see? I'm joshing you.

(**ALEX** *stands dumb.*)

Should I wait for your dad to come home?

ALEX. You can if you want, but he's usually out late.

(*pause*)

He's a heavy drinker. All the beatings have really made me worse for wear. So you know, when he gets here, keep your hands up.

COP. Your father sells advertising. That sort of person raises their child incorrectly in an entirely different way.

ALEX. Yeah? Well fuck you. I love my dad, bitch.

COP. He ran off without telling you where he was going.

ALEX. Nope. He's out, like I said.

COP. If I waited here until tomorrow morning, would I see him?

ALEX. I'd call the cops.

COP. I am the cops.

ALEX. I'd call Internal Affairs. You seen that movie?

COP. If I waited, would he come back?

ALEX. I don't know.

COP. Because you don't know where he is.

GORDON. (*to the audience*) I ate my dinner at the diner. I took a call from Caroline, who apologized. That, I knew, was proof that she had been contacted by the police. It occurred to me that I was acting like someone who had done harm to his wife.

(**SEAN** *and* **BRONWYN,** *elsewhere.*)

BRONWYN. Keeping myself myself. Being myself as I am. Being a woman with a certain name, with a certain life, who made certain choices. Whose family was so-and-so and that family raised their children with such-and-such values. A product. That's how we say it. A product of your environment. We sell products, we sell ourselves, we offer ourselves up for scrutiny. All these choices are not made, they are offered. Pick door A or door B. You can go to college if you want to, you have enough money. That's what it is. To be who I am. A series of doors. Pick A or B. That's how it is if you can't change. If you can't take care of your children, you will not learn how to. If you can't cry when something terrible happens, but you can cry at Kleenex commercials, in the end, you will find yourself empty and cold and that's not something you can decide.

(pause)

I cannot do anything. I could not. I could not do anything.

SEAN. Are you feeling better?

BRONWYN. Yes. I shouldn't be, but I am.

SEAN. I'm sorry you got hurt.

BRONWYN. Eventually I'll get used to it.

SEAN. Yes.

BRONWYN. Someday, I'll go home.

SEAN. Someday, you will. Someday, if you want to, you will.

BRONWYN. This is just kidnapping. That's all this is. Some sort of kidnapping.

SEAN. I'm in love with you.

(pause)

Whoever you are.

GORDON. *(to the audience)* The next day, after spending another night staring at the television in the motel, I found myself at *Prima Materia Books*. In front there were rows of oddball teas, dedicated to curing things like consumption and incontinence. It had that sickly smell you taste between your throat and nose. In the back, it was a ramshackle affair, mostly books about New Age mysticism, the sort of thing that had become unpopular after everyone voted for Ronald Reagan and forwent organic rice. It seemed more like the sort of place you'd find in Sedona, near the Vortexes, than up the creek from a factory and a few depressing hills.

(– *to* **SEAN** –)

My wife, I think, bought a book here once.

SEAN. We have lots of books.

GORDON. *Traveling to Montpelier.*

SEAN. That's an oldie. Did she like it?

GORDON. I don't know if she did. Do you remember someone buying that recently?

SEAN. From me? It's not really the sort of thing we'd sell here. But we're not the only bookstore in the area. Do you need a new one? She lost hers?

GORDON. No, I have hers.

(*pause*)

Her name is Bronwyn. Was. Is.

(*pause*)

Sort of a memorable name.

SEAN. I don't know her.

GORDON. You're sure.

SEAN. Yes. I don't know her.

(*pause*)

GORDON. My wife seems to have left me.

SEAN. Well, that's terrible news. I'll tell you one thing: I've been married myself four times.

GORDON. Just one day I came home and she wasn't there. No note or sign. Nothing. She disappeared. And the only thing I could think of was to come here.

(– *taking out the bookmark* –)

See this? You sell these here?

SEAN. We don't sell 'em. We give 'em away.

GORDON. You just stick them in books?

SEAN. They're bookmarks. So, of course.

GORDON. We live in Erie. Eight hours away. How did I get this? How did my wife get it? I'm not accusing you of anything, but how did she get it?

SEAN. Found it in a book? Hey…you're really distressed. I can see that. But I'm going to tell you, and I know we don't know each other, but I'll tell you anyway… you're going to get through this and everything is going to be all right. I have a very good feeling about that. And about you.

(He smiles.)

GORDON. I cheated on my wife.

SEAN. I've cheated on all four of mine. That doesn't mean I don't love them. Mind if I recommend a book to you? It really helped me.

GORDON. I would mind. Why isn't there any address on your bookmarks?

SEAN. I…well, obviously there should be. It's just sort of a running joke around here. Cornersville doesn't really have other places to be. There's the barbershop and there's Goode's Grocer, but that's actually just on the Abnerton side. There's Gray Wolf Copper. There's the woods, and some folks that live back in there. Most everything around here is Abnerton.

(pause)

There's only one house that is actually in Cornersville proper. Besides the factory, on Route 33, in front of the creek.

GORDON. *(to the audience)* There was, there is, only one house in Cornersville. Only one home. Dumb luck. Expert detective work. Convenience.

(SEAN turns and he is with BRONWYN, some time ago, elsewhere.)

BRONWYN. I was a clock. This hairy man with red wet eyes put me in a bag and brought me home and put me on his mantle, just above an imitation stone fireplace. His wife saw me and didn't think anything of it. Just one more little thing around the house. I don't know how she could have missed what was happening right in front of her. My wooden doors, my two hands, my little the mechanisms whirling, my cherry wood frame…I could see him looking at all the tiny parts as his wife droned on about the price of gasoline. I never felt so… Loved. When he was gone, I'd watch his wife read magazines and masturbate. Then he'd come home and go straight for me, smiling and making sure I was wound. After dinner, when she would wash up, he'd take me and then open up my doors and clean me gently. The first time I was frightened. I mean, I wasn't really a clock, I thought. What if, by opening me up, he'd kill me outright. But, instead of tiny organs, I could see my metal insides in his glasses. It was uncomfortable, the pipe and brush. I felt like I would burst out laughing or crying. But I couldn't get caught, so I settled into it, relaxed into it, for the sake of secrecy. By the third day my mind completely changed and even knew this process as relief.

(pause)

The hard part was leaving him.

GORDON. I drove the not-very-great distance between here and there. The house was as the man described. Because it was only around 3pm, the effect of happening upon it was not cinematic. Before I went in, I pulled out my wife's cell phone and called my son.

*(**ALEX** and **GORDON**, on the phone.)*

ALEX. Hey.

GORDON. Yeah?

ALEX. Hey.

GORDON. I'll be home soon.

ALEX. Got it.

GORDON. Are you all right?

ALEX. Yeah.

GORDON. Sorry I…left you at home.

ALEX. Well, it's not like you didn't leave any food.

GORDON. Is everything ok?

ALEX. No.

GORDON. No?

ALEX. I'm going to wind up in therapy and probably never have a happy marriage.

(pause)

GORDON. But otherwise.

ALEX. I'm spit-shined.

GORDON. Great. Be home soon.

ALEX. Fuck you.

GORDON. Bye.

COP. So…

ALEX. Yup that was him.

COP. Calling on…

ALEX. My mom's cell phone.

COP. From where?

ALEX. Didn't say.

(pause)

Am I going to wind up in foster care, because I think I'd rather be emancipated.

COP. Kids in foster care almost never graduate high school.

ALEX. That doesn't sound too tough then.

GORDON. *(to the audience)* I knocked once and then again and then rang the bell. It was unremarkable in every way. There was no light on, no car in the garage, no evidence of anyone coming to the door.

(pause)

A single car would periodically enter into view, on Route 33, plowing by at 85 miles per hour. I left no impression, and did not look like an intruder.

(pause)

I walked down the mail box. There was a little bit of mail in there. Mr. Sean Barclay. A man. Living alone. Somewhere remote. Near the bookstore.

(pause)

I wiped a little dandruff out of my eyebrows. I hear myself say...

(– to **BRONWYN** *–)*

I wish someone would dash out my brains with a fucking tire iron.

BRONWYN. It's amazing. It always is.

GORDON. That's horseshit.

BRONWYN. It's practically metaphysical. This is how you are when you're 'upset.' This. You actually get less... of whatever you are. If that's possible.

GORDON. Why did we move here?

BRONWYN. We have a back yard. Even people in *Iran* have backyards. We're living like people. Sure, it's hard to make friends with you frothing at the mouth all the time. But at least we could have a garden. At least, in the summer, we could see a tree and not think "Oh my God. It's a tree."

GORDON. Trees bore me.

BRONWYN. Please, please say that at the party.

GORDON. I embarrass you?

BRONWYN. No.

GORDON. You want a divorce?

BRONWYN. No.

GORDON. I want a divorce.

BRONWYN. You won't soon. Hang in there.

GORDON. I don't want a divorce.

BRONWYN. I know. I know you don't. You don't want to leave me.

(pause)

Does this look all right?

GORDON. It looks good. You always look good.

(*pause*)

How long have I been at this? Whatever it is I'm at?

BRONWYN. Forever. You'll never be finished with it.

GORDON. I wasn't always like this.

BRONWYN. Yes, you were.

GORDON. I wasn't. I wasn't. This *happened* to me. I feel like somewhere I took this new turn and just started heading north. Someday, we'll live in Nova Scotia. With the other people of Nova Scotia. And, finally, we'll be too old to go any further. And boats will look like death traps and the world will just cave into a big pit and we won't go anywhere, anymore, ever again.

BRONWYN. Alex will shove us off on a snow drift. To preserve seal meat.

GORDON. Doesn't that bother you?

BRONWYN. I think you should get dressed.

GORDON. I think you should disappear and never return. Leave me in whatever passes for peace.

(*pause*)

BRONWYN. ...and when we get there....

(*pause*)

Don't talk to me like that.

(*pause*)

...and when we get there you will be nice and you will, in fact, smile and be happy we're out of the house. You will tell everyone how funny and smart Alex is. That's what we do.

(*pause*)

I did not tattoo a number to your arm and ship you with your family to Erie, Pennsylvania. You are not being tortured. You will, therefore, be a man. About this. No matter how unnatural that may feel.

(*pause*)

You want a divorce.

GORDON. I do not want to go to a party. I do not want to be at a party.

BRONWYN. *This* is what it looks like. When you are desperate and sad and miserable.

GORDON. Yes.

BRONWYN. Your face does *exactly* that. That *nothing* that it does. Like your arm is asleep, starting with your eyes.

GORDON. What should I do? Beat my chest? Tear my hair out?

BRONWYN. You should think something and feel something. Once. You should let that happen to you. See what it's like.

(pause)

I don't find you *entirely* humiliating.

(pause)

What is completely satisfactory to me, completely, is the way in which you comb your hair.

GORDON. *(to the audience)* I started peering in the windows. Curtains drawn in the front, so maybe I'll try the back. There are, one might call them, shrubs. Not much. Most of the place is weeds. It looks like someone just dropped this house in an open field and left it there. When I get around the back, I see that there's the traditional mess. Mower left out to rust, hose all undone, the idea of a garden long since dead. A sliding glass door, which I find locked, but it does provide some unfettered access, at least visually, into the house.

(pause)

It looks like enough room for a family, and set up for one. I can see straight through the house. There are plates and light decorations. The bookshelves are full of photo albums. The television faces a comfortable couch. No pets. There's a calendar next to the telephone, but I can't read anything on it. Maybe one thing, a date circled in red. It's not today. The calendar is still opened to two months ago.

(pause)

GORDON. *(cont.)* Then, what looks like clutter on the floors begins to take some sort of shape. I see shoe laces, of different types, all laid out in what appears to be a line. What was undoubtedly the shoes that they once held together are piled into a large wicker basket. There's what appear to be dried orange peels in a jar, on the floor, and a bowl of what could only be sour milk next to the oranges. Other bric-a-brac is everywhere. A purple candle broken in half. A piece of lined paper, torn out of a notebook, alone, with nothing written on it. A box of kitchen matches. Three pieces of denim. Elmer's Glue.

(pause)

On the table, open and face down, a copy of *Traveling to Montpelier.*

*(***BRONWYN*** *and* ***SEAN***, *some time ago.)*

BRONWNYN. Take this away. It's making me see things. Why do you drink this swill?

SEAN. It's a nickel and a half. That's why.

BRONWYN. And three quarters.

(pause)

So I guess we can blame it all on Mr. Boston's Peppermint, can't we?

SEAN. Did you see?

BRONWYN. You made it look like it turned into a hat.

SEAN. I *did* turn it into a hat.

(pause)

Here's what I'm curious about. Not *why* it works, because I could never possibly understand. Not *why.* The question for me is…was this carrot always, deep down, a hat? Are all carrots hats? I mean, what do a carrot and a hat have in common? Is it more than we could possibly know? More than we could understand? Do carrots and hats walk hand in hand throughout the cosmos, winking at each other?

BRONWYN. The way we do?

SEAN. The way *they* do. The way *only* they can. Maybe.

(pause)

Because this really did happen, Winnie. This is what I'm trying to show you.

BRONWYN. I am not having another sip.

SEAN. There was a man who wondered, once, if a horse ever had all his hooves off the ground at once while running. The human eye, you see, can't know. Won't know without some aid. A horse's legs more too fast. So this man commissioned the invention of a device that could take hundreds of pictures of a horse running, and then play them back one by one. The horses movements were captured, repeatable, and in an instant the man could see.

(pause)

That was the invention of the moving image. The desire to know what was happening, and capture it. To study. Movies now are entertainment. But we watch things move, because it's impossible.

(pause)

I can turn this carrot into a hat. I can turn this bowl of milk into two different things, depending on which direction I stir. I can make it into a small leather strap, or a tooth. A molar. Why, you ask? Maybe something to do with the calcium. Maybe something to do with it being cow's milk. So there is a relationship. But why, why…does it work only when the milk is sour?

(pause)

Why are you looking at me like that?

BRONWYN. *(to the audience)* He told me that he'd never done it to a human being. Of course, I could understand why.

GORDON. *(to the audience)* I waited. What else was there to do?

BRONWYN. *(to the audience)* First of all, there's a sense of anticipation. Of course there was the lingering doubt. But because Sean didn't know which combination would make it happen to me, and because we could barely tell what was happening… there was this sense that it could happen at any time.

(pause)

I don't know what it's like to look at. It would probably make you throw up. First, I felt as if my eyes were being squeezed so tightly that the entire room became gigantic and stretched. As if all the space that my body can take up suddenly was packed together, more dense. Then, my skin tightened and became brittle. I couldn't feel anything at all, not even the motion of the air and I flew together, like a car in a compactor.

(pause)

My nose became a tin loop on which the rest of my features hung. Between eyes, roman numerals began to count off from twelve. My nostrils spewed forth three spindles, as if they lived up my sinuses, and they began to point to what were once my lips and ears. My hair fell out, and inside me, my heart stiffened and the beats were replaced by audible ticking, as if all my organs were designed to fit into a nursery rhyme.

(pause)

I could feel the soft metals and hard metals. Not all of me was wood and metal, though. Thick paper was here and there, and a few pieces of wire. I didn't know where it all went, anymore than I could show you with accuracy where my spleen is.

(pause)

Something that felt like a single wing burst out of my back. It was there, of course, so I could be wound up.

*(**SEAN** and **GORDON**, as before.)*

SEAN. It appears I'm not at home.

(pause)

Is there some reason you're just standing in front of my house?

GORDON. Is this your house?

SEAN. We've established that it isn't *your* house.

GORDON. So we have.

SEAN. Yes.

GORDON. And I'm standing in front of your house.

SEAN. Yes.

GORDON. Do other people live in your house?

SEAN. No.

GORDON. And there are no other houses around?

SEAN. Right.

GORDON. So why are we keeping our voices down?

(– to the audience –)

He took me inside.

(pause)

In another story, one with a happier ending, I did not wait for him. He never comes home. I drive away and am never seen again.

SEAN. *(to Gordon)* It's a sort of spell, you see? From a book called *Traveling to Montpelier.* That is how I turned your wife into a clock.

(GORDON *and* **BRONWYN,** *in* **SEAN**'s *house.)*

BRONWYN. Hello.

GORDON. Hello.

BRONWYN. You came looking.

GORDON. Yes.

BRONWYN. You're smarter than I thought.

GORDON. Breadcrumbs.

BRONWYN. You want me to come home.

GORDON. Yes.

BRONWYN. You love me that much?

GORDON. Yes.

BRONWYN. Why do you do things to make me leave you?

GORDON. I don't know.

BRONWYN. Well I've left you, now. Whatever you were doing, it seems to have worked.

(*pause*)

I won't be coming home. I live here now.

GORDON. What about Alex?

BRONWYN. He's your son. Whatever is wrong with you will always be wrong with him.

(*pause*)

I mean, honestly…what sort of person are you?

GORDON. I don't know.

BRONWYN. What are you even here for?

GORDON. I don't know.

BRONWYN. What use are you?

GORDON. I don't know.

(*pause*)

I can't tell…what I'm supposed to say.

BRONWYN. I know that.

(*A long pause. Something has been decided, or made clear.*)

GORDON. That man upstairs. Is he making you do anything you don't want to do?

BRONWYN. He isn't. I don't have much of a frame of reference. For what I want and what this is.

GORDON. What is this?

BRONWYN. I'm not sure.

(*pause*)

Did he tell you what I can do?

GORDON. How long have you known him?

BRONWYN. A long time.

GORDON. How long?

BRONWYN. Wait.

(She moves uncomfortably. Something is happening to her.)

Don't look.

GORDON. *(to the audience)* Evidently, whatever this man can do manifested itself without her permission. In front of me, suddenly, she changed.

SEAN. *(to GORDON)* I could turn her into any number of things. But a clock, that's what she is. *This* clock.

(He shows GORDON a miniature, antique, dusty, beautiful clock.)

Do you want to know how it's done?

GORDON. *(to the audience)* She begins in flakes and flecks. At first, they were like plumes of feathers, being shaken off. The more she moved, the more this downy dust flew away from her. Her clothes seemed to just flutter to the floor. Her legs curled up inside her, her arms wrapped backwards, her head lowered into her widening neck. All of this sounds so…thundering and bizarre. But it was graceful. Like origami.

(pause)

It didn't take long, but it felt like time stopped. I could feel things changing. Not just Bronwyn. The house we were in, this stranger's house, felt as if it was gone and we were below a field, looking up, at nothing. Or I was. If I was alone.

(pause)

She became wooden and golden. She became as far away as she could go. I coughed at the upturned skin and felt myself feeling sick. Her body was not solid, my body was not solid, we were not connected, we were flying separately into space.

(pause)

And then she was a tiny, beautiful clock. It looked like an antique, but it had just been born.

(pause)

Sean offers my wife to me for several thousand dollars. I want to beat him within an inch of his life, but I don't know how it works. I pay him for my wife.

(pause)

I spend another night at the motel with her. When I wake up, the police are there. They ask me why I drove away. I tell them, and I don't lie, that I was hoping to find my wife. I do lie about finding her.

*(**GORDON** takes a seat next to the **COP**, who "drives" him home. **GORDON** holds in his hands, now and for the rest of the play, the clock.)*

COP. *(to **GORDON**)* Let me tell you about being a parent. Parents cannot be sprinters. This is a long distance run. In fact, it's a series of long distance runs. Or a triathlon. It's a test of endurance and consistency, my friend. It is not about these little bursts. You can't suddenly show up, give the kid a bigger iPod and be a parent. You can't put Alex here in an expensive school, ask him how the day was, and expect him to treat his elders with a modicum of respect. Because that is not how it works, you see? Yes, yes, you're getting the standard lecture. You're getting the canned, do-not-turn-your-kid-into-Dylan-Klebold lecture. Because you know what? Kids like Alex, smart kids, they're the ones who know how to get tiny parts for handguns muled across the Canadian border in some unlucky Canuck's snatch. They're the kids who join message boards about creative mass ritual suicide. They're the ones who write anagrams with Charles Manson's name.

GORDON. *(to the audience)* He goes on like this. He never asks me again about my wife. He never asks me where I went. He just tells me that I shouldn't have gone anywhere.

ALEX. *(to the audience)* Fucking crazy shit goes down when you're just living your life, you know? A couple of days and my Dad pulls up to the front door, followed by the cop, who walks him in, nothing to say, and leaves him on the front porch. Dad has to whip out some keys. I didn't like, let him in because I was pissed. He knocked and all. I pretended not to hear him because I was pissed. He didn't say fuck all about Mom. He didn't say fuck all about anything. He gave me this shit he bought while he was on the road.

(pause)

It was pretty cool. What he got me. He never gets me shit that's not from Electronics Boutique.

(pause)

BRONWYN. *(to the audience)* I'm home. With my son. Sometimes I want to kiss him so badly that I almost turn back. But…not yet. Not yet.

(pause)

Gordon looks at me. Sometimes, when Alex is gone, he talks to me. He tell me he wants me to be myself again. He tells me stories about what he imagines. He tells me his pedestrian dreams. He walks me through our wedding.

(pause)

Sometimes, before he leaves the house, he will wind me ever so gently. Like when we first met.

GORDON. *(to the audience)* In the house, I rustle. I move, or am moved, between the rooms as if I running through them like water. I leave little evidences of me everywhere, but they are blown around by the tiniest movement. My foot drags on the floor, listing a little maybe, and the dust flutters. I molt and replace the skin that is dead, and remain myself. Appearances are not deceiving in my case: I cannot be what I am not. If I could shake hard enough, break off the feathers and atoms and let it all come loose, I'd let myself shake to bits. I'd leave no trace of me, not even a follicle. Whatever is left would be forgotten. My son would only notice that, in the summer, he feels clear-headed and calm. Not an itch or an inkling.

(pause)

There's no evidence of a crime.

(pause)

I will not go back and see Mr. Sean Barclay. I could be curious. But that is not the sort of man I am. She asked me what use I am. I am not of any use. There are things that I was shown, maybe, tricks. I can't tell. Maybe what I have in my house is not my wife at all. Maybe it was, but she is gone inside of it. Maybe she can't stay that way without oxygen. Maybe she can be like that forever. I can't understand, can't answer, and I am not curious. That is not what I'm good for.

SEAN. *(to the audience)* I'll read you a bit of the missing chapter:

"We tend to look at physics in terms of the very large and the very small. The movement of galaxies and the movement of quarks, that's what we believe will give us answers. I would argue that things as they are, invented, combined, apparently without unstable chemicals, can be combined and mixed and studied just as they are. We must think of the possible like the periodic table of elements. How many men must tie his shoelaces at once in order to make the sun turn into a block of ice? There is a number that adds up to this. There are a number of oranges we must eat, and there is a fruit that must be eaten next, if we are to invent an extra planet."

(pause)

How I make my living is my business.

GORDON. *(to the audience)* Late at night, after a day deriding downstairs Jim, making eggs and soup…I imagine she waits for me to close my eyes so that she can breathe and eat and kiss Alex on the head and call in whatever favors I owe her.

(pause)

When I am asleep, trees bow towards us when we walk together. The constellation Orion has ceased to exist.

Flies grow spontaneously from garbage and rotting meat. Genetic research invents a cabbage with the mind of a dolphin. My muscles atrophy. I sleep with a woman half my age. My son becomes a Catholic priest. I blow cumulonimbus clouds from the bottom of my lungs onto unsuspecting strangers. The earth's temperature suddenly becomes completely stable and refuses to change. Tick tock, says the nursery rhyme. She says that she likes the way I comb my hair.

(pause)

Everything else is the same. Until I turn out the lights and wait for her to come back. To come back to me.

(pause)

Until I turn out the lights.

(pause)

Like this.

(BLACK OUT)

OTHER TITLES AVAILABLE FROM SAMUEL FRENCH

GUTENBERG! THE MUSICAL!
Scott Brown and Anthony King

2m / Musical Comedy

In this two-man musical spoof, a pair of aspiring playwrights perform a backers' audition for their new project - a big, splashy musical about printing press inventor Johann Gutenberg. With an unending supply of enthusiasm, Bud and Doug sing all the songs and play all the parts in their crass historical epic, with the hope that one of the producers in attendance will give them a Broadway contract – fulfilling their ill-advised dreams.

"A smashing success!"
- The New York Times

"Brilliantly realized and side-splitting!
- New York Magazine

"There are lots of genuine laughs in Gutenberg!"
- New York Post

Lightning Source UK Ltd.
Milton Keynes UK
UKOW06f1057241116
288439UK00001B/1/P